SAINT FRANCIS OF ASSISI

Canticle of the Sun

❖

Most High, all-powerful, good Lord,
yours are the praises, the glory, the honour, and all blessing.
To you alone, Most High, do they belong,
and no man is worthy to mention your name.

Praised be you, my Lord, with all your creatures,
especially Sir Brother Sun,
who is the day and through whom
you give us light. And he is beautiful and radiant with
great splendour;
and bears a likeness of you, Most High One.

Praised be you, my Lord, through Sister Moon
and the stars;
in heaven you formed them clear and precious and
Beautiful.

Praised be you, my Lord, through Brother Wind,
and through the air, cloudy and serene, and every kind
of weather,
through which you give sustenance to your creatures.

Praised be you, my Lord, through Sister Water;
which is very useful and humble and precious
and chaste.

For Elise and Andrea
God's special gifts J.D.

For Lorenzo E.T.

Saint Francis of Assisi
2008 First Printing this Edition

Text copyright © 2007 Joyce Denham
Illustrations copyright © 2007 Elena Temporin
This edition copyright © 2007 Lion Hudson plc

ISBN 978-1-55725-571-6

The moral rights of the author and illustrator
have been asserted

Published in the United States by Paraclete Press, 2008.
Originally published in 2007 by Lion Hudson plc
Mayfield House, 256 Banbury Road,
Oxford OX2 7DH, England

1 3 5 7 9 10 8 6 4 2 0

Published by Paraclete Press
Brewster, Massachusetts
www.paracletepress.com

Typeset in 14/20 Elegant Garamond BT
Printed and bound in China

Saint Francis
of Assisi

Joyce Denham
Illustrated by Elena Temporin

PARACLETE PRESS
BREWSTER, MASSACHUSETTS

The Christening in Assisi

❖

LADY PICA POUTED. Her husband, Peter Bernardone, was still away in France buying lavish fabrics for their cloth shop in the little mountain town of Assisi, Italy. He had been gone for months, missing the birth of their son, and now the christening too.

'I wonder if Peter will ever see his child,' Pica sighed.

She carried her baby to the church. Bells rang in the tower. The rose-coloured walls of narrow stone houses sparkled in the sun – houses packed shoulder-to-shoulder on mountainside streets – streets so steep some were built as stone staircases. 'The whole world is rejoicing at my son's baptism,' Pica laughed.

'What is his name?' asked the priest.

'John,' said Pica, 'for John the Baptist.'

'Truly?' said the priest. 'John the Baptist loved God, but… he was also a wild man, who wandered the land without food or clothes of his own.'

'Yes, but he was God's wild man,' said Pica. 'And if my son grows to love God even half as much, he will be a good man.'

Weeks later, Peter came strutting through the door like a peacock, returning at last from his long shopping trip. 'I am in love with France!' he cried. 'France has made me rich!'

His eyes fell on his son.

'Ah, my little Frenchy!' he bellowed.

'His name is John,' said Pica.

'But my dearest love,' Peter reasoned, 'France is simply wonderful! Wait until I show you the new embroideries!'

'He is named after John the Baptist,' Pica said firmly.

'Nonsense!' said Peter. 'I shall call him *Francis* – my little Frenchy – to remind me of France.'

7

The French Troubadours

❖

FRANCIS GREW INTO a wild young man. He wore extravagant clothes: French clothes. He spent money on anything he wanted. The young nobles loved him because he paid for their drinking parties and led them on merry romps through Assisi, singing and calling and disturbing everyone in town.

'Where is Francis *now*?' Peter roared one day.

'Off with the other boys,' Pica answered.

'Again? He was out half the night with them, running in the streets, serenading that poor girl down the lane, singing in the market as if it were noontime. Today all of my customers complained about it. They know that Francis is the leader.'

That is why Francis had left his father's cloth shop unattended. His friends had dashed in exclaiming that two famous troubadours from France were performing in the square. Francis sprinted out the door, leading them to hear the poet-singers.

They sang of King Arthur and his Knights of the Round Table. Francis stood mesmerized.

This is the tale of Arthur,
High King of Britain's folk,
Who fought barbaric Saxons,
Who broke the tyrant's yoke.

'One day I, too, will be a knight!' Francis announced to everyone in the square. 'I will earn glory in battle, fighting for the oppressed.' Suddenly, he acted out an imaginary sword fight. 'Oh Francis, what will you think of next?' the crowd laughed.

He thought of the shop. Up the stone steps he darted, through the narrow lanes he bolted, until – breathless – he fell through the door.

'Francis,' Peter ordered, 'stop chasing around with those boys! You are a merchant's son. Your place is at work. Now!'

Secretly, though, Peter was very pleased that his own son was the preferred friend of the rich young nobles of Assisi.

The Beggar in the Shop

✣

A BUYER WAS eyeing the expensive English embroideries. Peter looked at Francis, as if to say, 'Go and help that customer, and make sure he buys something.'

Happily, Francis tempted the man with more of Peter's wares. There was deep blue wool, a length of fiery orange silk, then another of soft green linen. The man had never seen anything so striking. 'These are the finest of their weaves,' murmured Francis.

'Sir,' a voice quietly interrupted, 'will you help me?' Francis turned, but it was just a ragged old beggar asking for alms. Francis ignored him. After all, here was a wealthy, important aristocrat ready to make a large purchase.

The man was impressed. 'I will take all three for my lady,' he cooed, as he pressed a bag of gold coins into Francis' open palm. Francis clutched it, and felt the thrill of success.

He had not, however, forgotten the beggar – *could* not forget him. But when he turned to help him, the old man was gone.

Suddenly, Francis' heart felt heavier than the gold in his hands. *Would a true knight disregard the poor? Would a true knight not run to their rescue and defend them?*

Out the door he dashed. From shop to shop he ran. Up and down the crooked lanes he sprinted, seeking the elusive beggar. Finally, he spotted him sitting beside a fountain.

'Forgive me,' Francis pleaded. 'I do want to help you.' Then he pressed the bag of coins into the man's hand and ran away.

A new joy bubbled up inside of Francis – a joy much greater than that of making money. He sang and danced all the way home, and he vowed, right then and there, that he would never again refuse to help the poor.

The Duke Decides

❧

'F IRE!' The shouts echoed from every terrace. Townsfolk ran frantically up the steep lanes. They carried weapons: swords, clubs, even stones. The castle, perched high on the mountain, was burning, and smoke draped itself like a coarse dark wool over the topsy-turvy roofs of Assisi. 'What is happening?' asked Francis.

'The townspeople have rebelled against the duke,' said Peter. 'He does not care about us.'

'They will drive him out today – ' Pica prophesied, ' – the duke and his entire German garrison!'

She was right. The duke and every one of his soldiers fled the burning castle. The nobles who had forced the common people to work as their slaves also fled – to the town of Perugia. That very day, the Assisi merchants banded into a community of tradesmen who could govern and protect the town themselves.

'Come on!' they shouted. 'Take the stones from the castle… we'll build a wall all around Assisi so that no cruel duke can ever besiege us again!' Francis hefted large stones; he pretended he was one of Arthur's knights working to free the oppressed villagers. The masons showed him how to build stones into a high wall. It was the first time in his life that he had done hard, physical work. It satisfied him. He grew strong. And as the stones were fastened one to another, the bond of loyalty between the citizens of the little mountain town grew strong and solid as well. They cared for each other.

Is it possible that God is more like the community than like the duke? Francis wondered.

The Battle Resumes

A FEW YEARS LATER, the duke's nobles who had fled to Perugia declared war on Assisi.

Peter and Pica watched the Assisian army march down the mountain to the wide plain below. Peasant foot soldiers went first; behind them rode knights on armoured horses. The knights let Francis ride with them, and Peter thought how fine his son looked in his new armour. Pica wept and prayed… and thought about John the Baptist.

On the banks of the River Tiber, the Perugians slaughtered the Assisians. But they spared the knights – who were wealthy and might be ransomed by their families – and locked them in a dungeon. Francis, too, was imprisoned.

'We'll never see our families again! We'll rot in here!' the knights moaned. Francis decided to sing.

This is the tale of Francis,
Assisi's bravest knight;
God sent him to the people
To aid them in their plight.

'You're crazy, Francis!' his fellow prisoners shouted. 'How can you sing such nonsense when you're locked in this dungeon?'

'I can and I will,' said Francis, 'because when I'm free, I will become a famous knight. The whole world will know my name!'

An entire year went by, during which Francis kept singing and planning his future glories. Then, one day, the guard unlocked the door and let the bony, starving men go. They had been ransomed.

'Francis!' Peter waddled out to greet his son. 'Now that you're back, we'll be richer than ever! No one sells cloth as well as you!'

The Impoverished Knight

✤

'Look!' said Peter one day, as a soldier rode past their shop. 'He is going to fight with Gautier de Brienne, to defeat the armies of the German emperor.'

'The troubadours all sing of the glories of Gautier de Brienne, the greatest knight of all,' said Francis. 'I too will fight under his banner!'

'No,' Peter protested. 'You are needed here – in our shop – where every day you earn glory by the profits you bring in.'

'I have not spent a year in prison only to waste my days selling cloth,' Francis insisted. 'If I can help de Brienne defeat the Germans, I will be knighted on the battlefield. Everyone in Italy – in the whole world – will know that Francis Bernardone brought glory to his country.'

Although Peter continued to argue, he also began to imagine his son riding into battle with the nobles and he soon placed a large bag of gold in Francis' hand.

Francis bought the strongest, most spirited horse; he was measured for a hauberk, boots and a helmet. Riding back home, he rounded a bend and saw a poor knight watering his skinny old horse at a fountain. Francis stopped cold. 'Where does your journey take you?' he asked.

'To fight with Gautier de Brienne.'

'Dressed like that?'

'It is all I have left,' the man answered.

'But you have no armour, no helmet, no shirt even,' Francis moaned.

Quickly, he wriggled out of his newly sewn tunic and handed it to the surprised knight. He put his own boots on the man's feet and draped his red-embroidered cloak over the shivering man's back.

'But… I cannot repay you,' the knight stammered.

'You already have,' said Francis, 'for when I saw you, I felt the love of God rising in my heart.'

He looked so much like Jesus, Francis thought as he rode away.

The Dream of a Lifetime

❖

WEEKS LATER, Francis left to become a knight. He sat pressed into his new saddle, his long coat of chain mail hanging like a dead weight from his shoulders. A young squire rode obediently behind him on another, slightly smaller horse.

With a chivalrous air, Francis galloped out of Assisi, never glancing back at its safe, encompassing wall – the wall that he himself had helped to build. They camped for the night at Spoleto. But Francis couldn't sleep. He gazed at the bright moon while dark thoughts of battle tugged at his heart. Suddenly, he felt as weak as when he had emerged from the cruel dungeon. His head nodded, his eyelids slowly drooped, and the moon… vanished.

'Francis, where are you going, all dressed up in such costly armour?' a voice asked.

'I am going to fight the Germans under the banner of Gautier de Brienne,' he answered.

'You are only seeking the servant. Why not seek the master?'

'Dearest Lord,' Francis cried, 'what do you want me to do?'

'Return to your town,' the voice told him, 'and I will show you.'

Francis woke, and there was the moon, still shining. For the rest of the night he pondered his dream, which had ended all of his desire to go into battle.

In the morning, he turned and went back to Assisi. Back through the town gates. Back up the winding lanes with his snorting steed and his humiliated squire.

'Look! Here comes Francis, back already!' the townsfolk jeered. 'Here comes the brave knight with his battle wounds,' they laughed.

Francis was not embarrassed. 'I've come back because I was called to a greater purpose,' he announced. 'Just you wait and see.'

The Cave

AFTER HIS NIGHT-TIME adventure, Francis lost all interest in selling cloth. Sad and confused, he walked the hills, wondering what God was trying to tell him. 'My teachers say that God is an angry dictator – like the German emperor, or the old duke,' he said aloud to the birds, who seemed to listen to him. 'Yet when I see God's beautiful creation, I see love. What can this mean?'

One day, Francis discovered a little cave in the mountainside and crawled into it. But his soul was crawling into an even darker cavern. 'My life is so empty,' he wept. 'I have wasted my youth on foolish parties and rich clothes, and now I am tortured by guilt. Is God punishing me?' he cried. 'Will God forgive me?'

Francis sat in the dark cave for days. There, he recalled his long year chained in the black, rat-infested dungeon, where an unexplainable joy had flooded his heart and he could sing. That joy was a miracle from God! he realized.

He thought of the beggar in his father's shop and the unexpected compassion he felt for him. Surely that, too, came from God!

Finally, he thought of the half-naked, shivering
knight who reminded him of Jesus. Suddenly Francis
understood: Jesus lived in poverty to befriend the poor and
sick, and to show the world that *God is love*.

Francis leapt from the dark and gloomy cave. 'God is not a tyrant!'
he shouted to the sky. 'God is our friend! The only true friend of the poor,
the sick, the lonely and the imprisoned.

'I am no wealthy man's knight,' he proclaimed. 'I am Christ's knight!'

'If you are a knight, then who is your lady?' shouted a friend, approaching him.

'Her name is Poverty,' Francis called back. 'And I shall embrace her with all my
heart, just as Jesus did. With her by my side, I will show the world that God is love.'

The Pilgrimage to Rome

❖

'I AM GOING ON pilgrimage to Rome,' Francis announced.
'I forbid it!' Peter snarled. Francis went anyway – all dressed up in a green silk cloak and a bright yellow tunic. But he walked, so as not to waste money on a horse.

The plaza in front of St Peter's tomb was jammed with pilgrims and beggars. One of the beggars eyed Francis' expensive clothes and pleaded, 'Will you help me, rich man? Will you?'

What a fool I've been, thought Francis. 'Quick!' he ordered the man. 'Give me your clothes and take my own.'

'But mine are only rags!' the beggar said in disbelief.

'Exactly,' Francis answered. They swapped clothes. Then Francis, now barefoot and smelly, began his long walk home.

But why did the journey seem so easy? Why did he feel so free? 'Because I have acted as Christ's knight,' he sang, 'and for the first time in my life, I have everything I need.'

Assisi was already in sight when an awful stench wafted across the narrow road. A small bell rang: clink… clink… clink. Francis panicked. Around the bend came a foul, disfigured leper, shaking his clapper to warn people away. 'Ach!' Francis gagged, and he ran as fast as he could in the other direction. At last he stumbled, fell over in a heap and wept, clutching at his filthy rags. 'How many times have I been told to shun the poor and the sick,' he sobbed, 'as if they suffer from God's judgment. But look at me, as poor and putrid as that leper. If God loves me, surely God loves him too.'

He ran back to find the man. 'Forgive me!' he called, spying him beside the road. 'Forgive me for shunning you. I want to be your friend, just as God is.' Then he took the bent and lonely old man in his arms and kissed him.

Tears ran down the leper's worn face. 'No one has touched me in twelve years,' he wept, his own heart touched by such kindness.

The Church of San Damiano

❖

FRANCIS STAGGERED through the door, exhausted from his pilgrimage. 'No cloak and no shoes?' Peter sneered. 'Do you think the townspeople will shop here if you are in rags? Get out, until you are dressed properly!'

Francis obeyed, but he still had no interest in selling cloth. He was, after all, Christ's knight. But where, he wondered, was his battleground? These were his thoughts as he walked one day past the crumbling old church of San Damiano. He slipped into the tiny chapel and knelt before a painted wooden crucifix, now chipped and peeling. Suddenly, it seemed to speak to him.

'Rebuild my house,' Jesus said, 'for it has fallen into ruins.'

Francis surveyed the sorry state of San Damiano. 'That's it!' he exclaimed. 'As Christ's knight, I will repair these damaged walls!' Faster than he had ever run before, he sprinted home, harnessed his father's horse, loaded it with rolls of rich Chinese silks and Egyptian cottons, then galloped full speed to the market in Foligno – where he sold everything, including the horse.

Back at San Damiano, he handed the old priest a bag of gold – the gold from the sale. 'Oh, Francis,' the man chided, 'is this another one of your wild antics?'

'No,' Francis assured him. 'I want to repair the walls of this church.'

'But Francis, your father will be furious! This is his money; I dare not take it.'

Tossing the sack of gold into a corner, Francis begged the priest: 'Then at least permit me to sleep here. For I should not go home – not now, at any rate.'

Peter's wrath burned against his son. He hunted for him, and Francis ran away in terror. Deep in the forest he dug a hole and crouched in it, unseen. For an entire month he lived there until he was so thin and weak he could endure it no longer. He knew he must face his father. Yet he did not go unarmed. He had prayed for courage – a knight's courage – and God had granted it.

Up the streets of Assisi Francis staggered, dirty, unshaven, all skin and bones. Boys threw rocks at him. '*Pazzo! Pazzo!*' they shouted. 'Crazy man! Crazy man!' Francis kept walking until he stood at the door of his father's house.

'Where is my horse?' Peter demanded. 'Where are the bolts of silk and cotton?' he raged. 'What have you done?!'

'Father,' Francis tried desperately to explain, 'I want to serve God. I want to rebuild San Damiano.' Peter heard none of it. He beat Francis mercilessly, dragged him down the steps to the house dungeon, and locked him inside.

'Pica,' he wheezed, 'leave him there until I return.' Then Peter set off on one of his many business trips.

Pica talked with Francis through the barred door. He told her all about what he had learned in the cave, about Lady Poverty – his new love – and about the beggar in Rome, and the leper along the road. Finally, he told her about the voice from the crucifix in San Damiano. 'Mother,' he told her, 'I must rebuild Christ's house.'

Sweeter words Pica had never heard. 'Of course you must, *John*,' she whispered happily. Then she unlocked the door, gave Francis food and money, and blessed him in God's name as he went once again to the little church.

When Peter returned and discovered that Pica had let Francis go, he ran into the street in a fury. 'Come!' he shouted to his neighbours. 'Come! Help me capture my thieving son!'

When the noisy crowd arrived at San Damiano, Francis met them and calmly announced that he had left home for good. 'There is your money,' he told Peter, pointing to the corner where the sack of gold still lay.

'Seize him!' Peter cried. 'He must be punished!' So the group seized him and marched him to the bishop's palace where Peter stated his case against his son.

'Francis,' the bishop said, 'although you meant well, you have stolen property from your father, and that is wrong.'

Suddenly, a sparkle appeared in Francis' dark eyes. 'I happily return to Peter Bernardone everything I have that is his,' he said. Then he stripped off all his

clothes – all bought by Peter's wealth – and handed them to his father. The crowd gasped: Francis stood before them stark naked.

'From now on,' he declared, 'I serve only my heavenly Father; from now on, I want only the wealth of God's friendship.'

Bishop Guido rushed to his side, threw his cloak around Francis and hurried him away.

Peter never spoke to his son again.

With a lighter heart, Francis found a scratchy brown robe that had been worn by the bishop's gardener, put it on and tied a rope around his waist as a belt. Bishop Guido shook his head in wonder. 'You know,' he smiled, 'you are so wild in your love for God, you remind me of John the Baptist.'

The Friars

FRANCIS FINISHED rebuilding San Damiano. He had a lot of help because many people joined in the effort. They were amazed that the boy who sang so beautifully, and ran dancing and partying through the streets at night, who displayed so much wealth by his clothes, had now embraced poverty and was singing about God's love. Everyone wanted to be near him.

'A truer knight I have never seen,' one man said to another as they hauled stones.

'Yes,' his friend answered. 'His manners are noble. He is kind to the old and the weak; he even gives what little food he has to the hungry.'

'He is so full of joy,' added another.

Francis soon realized that it was not just San Damiano that God wanted him to rebuild, but the entire family of creation. People needed to hear that God is love.

Some men permanently joined Francis' mission. They, too, put on brown robes and wore no shoes. They gave up everything they had to befriend the poor and to imitate the life of Jesus.

'We shall call ourselves *friars*,' Francis told them, 'which means *brothers*. In the villages we will sing and preach about God's love and live on the food people share with us. We will be God's troubadours!'

Sometimes, as the friars sang, Francis pretended to accompany them on a violin. He sawed his imaginary bow over the strings with exaggerated motions; he danced all over the square as he played. People laughed and danced with him.

Francis bravely led his friars just as good King Arthur led his Knights of the Round Table. Eventually, hundreds joined the mission. All over France and Italy they spread – the Franciscan Friars – doing just what Francis taught them to do: living in poverty so that people could see the life of Jesus and the immense love that overflowed from God's own heart.

Sister Clare

✤

CLARE, A BEAUTIFUL young noblewoman of Assisi, had been listening to Francis. 'For weeks now,' she told her cousin Pacifica, 'he has preached in the cathedral. Never have I heard such words. He speaks of God as our lover. He sings songs about the the sun and the moon praising their creator. He tells us that the birds and the flowers, even the winds, are our brothers and sisters, because God made us all.'

'I like his piercing dark eyes,' Pacifica answered.

'You're not listening!' Clare chided. 'I'm talking about his *words*. Through them I have fallen in love with God!'

'And now your eyes are on fire, just like his.'

'Can you keep a secret?' Clare asked.

'For you, Clare, always,' Pacifica replied.

'I, too, want to live as Francis does, imitating Jesus. I know my parents will never permit it, for they love their wealth, and they want me to marry a rich man. So tomorrow night, when everyone is asleep, you must help me go to St Mary's, where Francis and the brothers will meet us. There I will take a vow of poverty and dedicate my life to God just like them.'

The moon shone on the small forest clearing behind St Mary's of the Angels. Squirrels woke; owls chanted *hoo… hoo*; and merry stars sparkled in the sky as the friars sang hymns of praise to the creator of all things. Deep in the shadows, where no one could see, Clare removed her elegant gown and slipped into a plain brown robe.

Then she stepped into the clearing, knelt down and uttered her vow to live in poverty and never to marry, so that she could devote all her days to prayer and helping the poor. At that, Francis lifted her long, thick tresses – the beautifully brushed hair of a rich lady – and cut them off.

Suddenly, torches lit up the forest. There were shouts: 'Stop her! We order you!' But her father's men had arrived too late.

Clare showed them her shaved head. 'This is the only marriage I want – ' she said, ' – to love God and to serve the poor all my days.' And that is exactly what she did.

The Sermon to the Birds

SOMEWHERE ALONG a rough track in Italy, Francis walked. As he walked, he preached. As he preached, people followed him. They wanted to hear everything he said.

At first, he seemed to be addressing the sky. 'Everything in creation is related,' he proclaimed. Then he looked down and spoke to worms crawling in the road. 'We are all brothers and sisters because all things are made by our loving God.'

In the nearby meadow, birds gathered. Hundreds of them, of every size and colour – larks, sparrows, cranes and crows – swooping and chattering and chirping. When Francis saw them, he called, 'Hello, sister birds!' Then he strode happily into the tall grasses of the field, while all around him the birds flocked. Some sat on his shoulders. One sat right on top of his head and sang so loudly, Francis laughed and sang with her.

'You birds,' he told them, 'must never cease to praise your creator. For when you do, you give glory to the God who loves each one of you.' They folded their wings and listened to the tones of Francis' kind voice.

'God gives you the glories of flight, letting you soar free above the earth. God clothes you in the most beautiful colours. You can neither spin nor weave, yet no cloth merchant in Europe can match your spectacular garments!

'And do not forget to thank God for your food, which you have in abundance. And for the clear, cold water of the mountain streams. All of these gifts are evidence of God's great love for you.'

For a long time the birds remained with Francis. He talked and they sang, and all of them seemed to be rejoicing together over the fact that God was their friend.

The friars, watching this scene from the road, were continually amazed at Francis' love for all things in creation. He understood the animals, even the tiniest bugs, and they had no fear of him.

'He is like Adam,' the brothers agreed.

Francis Rescues the Turtle Doves

❖

BACK AT THE FRIARS' HOME, Francis spoke to the gardener. 'Brother,' he said, 'you must stop tilling the edges of our fields. The wild flowers need a place to grow. Let them take root there, for they exist to praise their creator.'

Just then, a boy passed by carrying a cage full of wild turtle doves.

'Where are you taking those doves?' Francis asked.

'To market,' said the boy. 'I trapped them. They'll sell for good money.'

'Please,' Francis begged with tears in his eyes, 'they are so innocent. Give them to me instead.'

The boy was so surprised by Francis' love for the turtle doves that he gave him the entire cage of birds.

Francis held the frightened creatures in his lap. 'Why did you let the boy catch you?' he gently scolded. 'You are such special birds – a dove found dry land for Noah after the flood; a dove rested on Jesus' shoulder after his baptism. God has saved you from death because you teach us about God's grace. Come, I will help you build new nests.'

Francis collected sticks and grasses. He wove them into soft, round beds and placed them in safe nooks in the tree branches. 'There you are!' he said. 'Now you may sing and multiply as God intended.' Francis fed them; he sang them little songs; and the gentle doves sang back.

All the while, the boy who had trapped the birds watched in amazement.

'One day,' Francis told him, 'you will join our order of brothers.'

The boy never forgot what he saw that day. As soon as he was grown, he became a friar and spent the rest of his life serving the poor in Christ's name, just as Francis had served the poor, helpless turtle doves.

The Wolf of Gubbio

❖

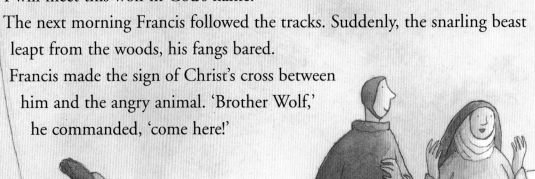

I<small>N THE TOWN</small> of Gubbio, there lived a ravenous wolf.

'He kills our sheep and our cows,' the people told Francis. 'He even attacks *us*! We live in constant terror.'

'I will talk with this wolf,' Francis declared.

'No!' they shouted. 'Do not do such a foolish thing!'

'It is God's will,' said Francis, 'that all creatures may live together in peace. I will meet this wolf in God's name.'

The next morning Francis followed the tracks. Suddenly, the snarling beast leapt from the woods, his fangs bared.

Francis made the sign of Christ's cross between him and the angry animal. 'Brother Wolf,' he commanded, 'come here!'

Cautiously, the wolf approached.

'Brother Wolf,' Francis said, 'you will not hurt me and you will never again hurt any human or animal. God has not given you permission to harm the creation.'

At these words, the wolf lowered his head in submission. 'Today you must make peace with the people of Gubbio,' Francis continued. 'I know you did your evil deeds because you were hungry. The people will forgive you and I will instruct them to feed you every day for the rest of your life. You will never need to kill anything again. Now then, give me a sign that you accept this treaty.'

The wolf followed Francis back to the town square and there, with all of the villagers watching, he placed his paw in Francis' outstretched hand.

'Hooray!' the children cried. 'The hungry wolf is tamed!'

The old creature lived for two more years, going quietly from house to house in Gubbio, and each morning and each night the residents gave him his day's food. When he finally died, they grieved deeply. 'He made Gubbio into the Garden of Eden,' they wept, 'where people and animals lived together in peace and friendship.'

Francis and the Sultan of Egypt

❖

'THERE CAME AN even more ravenous wolf: War.

Knights from all over Christian Europe were fighting in the Middle East, trying to recapture Jesus' birthplace from the Moslems. In truth, many knights joined the war only for adventure – to torture, kill and plunder.

'This crusade is not holy,' said Francis. 'People made in God's image must never kill each other. I will go to the Moslem Saracens myself and tell them about the true peace of Christ.'

'No!' Cardinal Pelagio warned him. 'They will kill you! The sultan pays his warriors in gold for the heads of Christian soldiers.'

'I am Christ's knight,' said Francis, 'fighting for peace with the weapons of love and truth.' He soon set sail for Egypt with Brother Illuminato.

They walked straight to the enemy camp. Suddenly, Moslem warriors sprang at them from behind. Their captors beat them, bound them in chains and dragged them to Sultan Malik-al-Kamil.

'Why are you here?' he demanded.

'To tell you about the love of Christ,' Francis answered.

Malik-al-Kamil and Francis soon became friends. They both loved talking about God. 'How can I know that your words are true?' the sultan asked him.

'I will pass through fire to prove it,' Francis volunteered. 'If I survive, then you will know you have heard God's words.'

'I cannot consent to such a test,' Malik-al-Kamil said. 'But you must visit me often, and because you are a holy man I ask you to pray for me, that I may know God's will.'

Malik-al-Kamil granted Francis safe passage when he left. He also presented him with a special gift – a horn, that Francis used to call people together when he preached back in Italy – just as the Moslems called their people together for prayer many times each day.

Francis was the only knight who single-handedly tried to end the war – by talking rather than by fighting.

The First Christmas Creche

IT WAS CHRISTMAS time, and Francis had an idea.

'This year,' he told his friend John Velita, lord of Greccio, 'I want to celebrate the birth of Jesus in a special way – a way that helps people understand how he came from the splendour of heaven to this poor earth.'

'It will be one of your plays, won't it?' said John, clapping his hands in excitement.

'Yes,' said Francis, 'and I will need to use one of the caves on your mountainside.'

'It is yours,' said John. 'What will you need?'

'Animals – an ox, a donkey and some sheep. And a manger filled with hay for the animals' feed.'

John got everything ready, and Christmas Eve arrived under a clear, starlit sky. Sister Moon's shimmering white path led straight up the mountain to the little manger. From all over they came – villagers, with blazing torches – to hike the cold, steep path to the cave… and there it was: the stable of Bethlehem, recreated before them.

'Oh!' they gasped in reverent awe.

There between the ox and the donkey stood Francis. 'This is where Jesus was born; this is where he slept, here in this manger,' Francis said, his voice breaking with emotion. 'Here is where the Lord of the universe arrived, as a helpless infant, surrounded by animals and dusty hay.'

Softly, the friars began to sing; and the stone echoed back their plain tones in that dark chamber. 'A host of angels appeared in the sky,' Francis explained, 'singing *Glory to God in the highest; peace on earth!*'

Then, as the villagers peered into the simple little manger, they lifted their torches high and the cave filled with a warm, golden light. 'Even so,' said Francis, 'Jesus came as the Light of the World, bearing God's love.'

The Stigmata

❖

T HE NEXT SPRING, Francis went
all alone to his favourite
mountain retreat. He was very ill
and nearly blind. But the craggy
mountaintop of La Verna filled him with joy.
Up there, he could feel Brother Wind; he could hear
Sister Stream; he could wrap himself in the warmth of Brother Sun.
And every evening, a falcon flew to Francis' hut and joined him for evening prayer.

Soon it was September. Leaves turned gold and red, and the warm, scented air of
day yielded to cold, crisp nights. 'Brother Falcon,' Francis said wearily, 'I am near
the end of my journey on this earth. Soon I will be in heaven.'

Day and night he prayed. More than ever he longed to imitate
Christ's life. 'Dearest Lord,' he cried, 'I have one wish: As I have
known the love of Jesus, so may I also know his sufferings.'

Early the next morning, before the sun burst over the rocky
summit, Francis lay on the ground, weak and in pain. His
diseased eyes hurt so badly he could not open them. And yet he
saw the most marvellous vision: a heavenly angel, with flaming
wings stretched out in the shape of a cross.

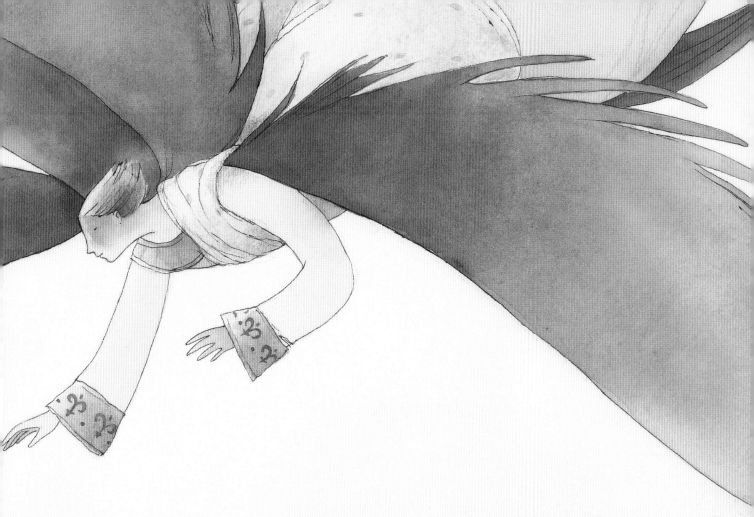

'The angel of Christ!' Francis whispered. Swiftly it flew over him, looked into his poor, hurting eyes, and disappeared.

'Brother Falcon!' Francis exclaimed, 'look at my hands and feet.' They were scarred, as if by nails. Miraculously, Francis had received the wounds Jesus suffered when he was crucified by the Romans – the wounds he bore because God so loved the world.

Two years later, Francis Bernardone – whose real name was *John* – died, having shown the world that God is our very best friend. He was forty-six, and that was a ripe old age for a knight.

The Call to Repentance

❖

Bless and praise the Lord God.
Thank and adore the Almighty –
the three in one: Father, Son and Holy Spirit,
who created all that exists.
Confess your faults without delay,
for you do not know how long you may live.
If you give, you will receive;
if you forgive, you will be forgiven.
Be on your guard, and turn away from evil.
Do good until the end of your days.

ALSO FOR CHILDREN FROM PARACLETE PRESS

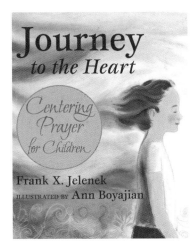

Journey to the Heart

$14.95
32 pages
Large full-color paperback

Many books have been published that teach adults the practice of centering prayer. Finally, a guide for children!

"A wonderful invitation to children of all ages to enter into contemplative prayer and find inner peace, much needed in our troubled world. We can trust that God will work in these 6-minute silent prayer times. This is an outstanding opportunity to offer children."
–GAIL FITZPATRICK-HOPLER, Director, Contemplative Outreach Ltd.

"Journey to the Heart tells you God is with you and loves you. Just remember God brought you to life so you should care and love Him too. Take time to pray with Him as I do."
–AUSTIN HOPLER, 9 years old

This resource has been given the Nihil Obstat by William B. Smith, S.T.D. and the Imprimatur by Dennis J. Sullivan, Vicar General, Archdiocese of New York.

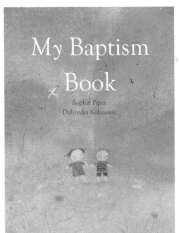

My Baptism Book

$14.95
64 pages
Hardcover with ribbon marker

This inspiring and lovely book makes the perfect gift for any child and his/her family on the day of Baptism or First Communion.

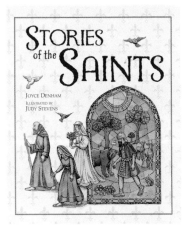

Stories of the Saints

$9.95
48 pages
Large full-color paperback

Also by Joyce Denham, this colorful book presents the stories of 14 of the great saints of Christian tradition. An ideal resource for educators, parents, Sunday school teachers, librarians, and everyone else who cares about communicating the history and spirit of the saints to today's elementary school-age children.

Available from most booksellers or through Paraclete Press:
www.paracletepress.com; 1-800-451-5006.
Try your local bookstore first.